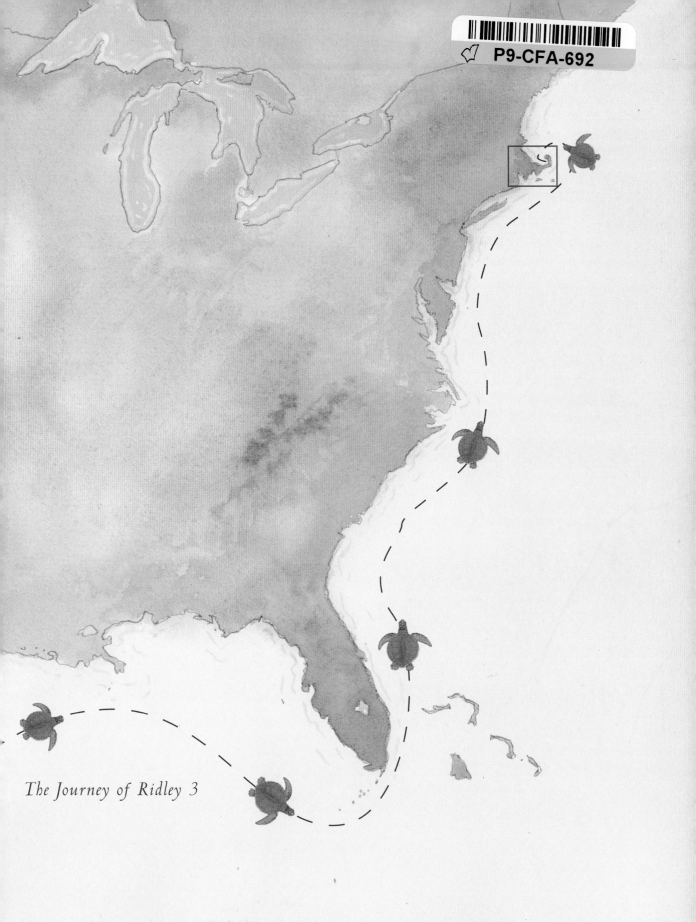

The Journey of Ridley 3

Every
Turtle
Counts

by Sara Hoagland Hunter

illustrated by Susan Spellman

Peter E. Randall Publisher
Portsmouth, New Hampshire
2014

Distributed by
University Press of New England

ISBN: 978-1-931807-25-8
Library of Congress Control Number: 2013949756

Published by
Peter E. Randall Publisher
Box 4726
Portsmouth, NH 03802
www.perpublisher.com

Distributed by
University Press of New England
www.upne.com

Book design: Grace Peirce
www.nhmuse.com

"Autism made school and social life hard,
but it made animals easy."

—Temple Grandin, animal scientist,
professor, and best-selling author

For Tessa and Gigi
SS

For my niece, Mimi, whose unfiltered joy and affection
expand our spectrum. You have never rescued a sea turtle but,
like Mimi in this tale, you have great gifts to share.
SHH

There were others who walked the beach that day, but only one who stopped to look.

And she made all the difference.

Mimi chased the birds across the frozen sand, chanting the words she loved so well, "Eider duck, herring gull, tern, merganser! Eider duck, herring gull, tern, merganser!"

When a wave crashed at her feet and licked her boots, she galloped
into the dune grass and crouched, shaking.

"It's all right, Mimi!" shouted her mother.

Mimi hugged her knees, rocked, and repeated, "It's all right, Mimi.
It's all right, Mimi."

When her mother reached for her hand, Mimi hugged her knees even
tighter. "I've brought you a bucket," said her mother. "There's sure to
be treasure if we look hard enough!"

Mimi grabbed the bucket. "Sure to be treasure," she repeated.

She crawled along the dark line of seaweed, shells, and
washed-up bottles. First, she found a necklace full of tiny shells.

"A mermaid's necklace," said Mother, reaching to place it around her neck.

Mimi frowned and pulled away.

When the bucket overflowed with crab claws, clam shells, and fish netting, Mother said it was time to go home. But Mimi ran in the other direction.

"Hurry, now! We'll be late for dinner!" called her mother.

But Mimi ran and ran. She ran so fast, she tripped and fell.

"Are you all right?" called her mother.

But Mimi didn't answer. She was too busy staring at two black eyes staring back at her.

"Don't touch! It's dirty!" shouted her mother, pulling hard on her sleeve.

But Mimi didn't listen. She picked up the turtle and cradled it in her arms.

"Put that thing down!" begged her mother. "It's time to go! Mrs. Sims is coming for dinner."

When Mimi wouldn't budge, her mother sighed, picked up both her and the turtle, and carried them off the beach.

"Dead," said the fisherman at the town wharf.

"Dead as a doornail," agreed
the harbormaster.

"That thing is not coming in my
house," said Mrs. Sims, the landlady.
"It stinks to high heaven!"

"Come, Mimi," urged Mother. But Mimi hugged the turtle closer and would not come in the house. While they ate dinner, Mimi sat on the steps and hummed to her new friend.

Mrs. Sims phoned the Massachusetts Audubon Society. "I need you to remove this filthy thing from my home."

Mr. Prescott, the Audubon man, arrived quickly and unloaded a crate from his van. "You did just the right thing keeping the turtle outside," he said to Mimi.

Mimi hid her head.

"That's a Kemp's ridley, the rarest sea turtle on earth. They hatch on just one beach in the world—down in Mexico."

"What are they doing all the way up here?" asked her mother.

Mr. Prescott brushed sand from the turtle's back. "Nobody knows for sure. It's only the young ones who stray this far. When the cold weather hits, they can't figure out how to go south. They get trapped in the hook of Cape Cod."

"And die," snapped Mrs. Sims.

Mimi stomped her feet and covered her ears.

Mr. Prescott stepped closer. "Not necessarily," he said. "Some are just cold-stunned." He reached out for the turtle. "But I can't tell until I thaw them out a little. It's a good thing you rescued this turtle and kept it outside. A frozen turtle shouldn't thaw too fast."

"Shouldn't thaw too fast," repeated Mimi.

Mimi loosened her grip and let Mr. Prescott lift the turtle into the crate.

"Well, you may as well give up," said Mrs. Sims. "This one's definitely dead."

"I never give up on a turtle," he said. "Every turtle counts."

Mimi looked up for the first time and smiled. "Every turtle counts," she repeated.

"What are its chances?" whispered Mother.

"About the same chance it had to make it through sharks, shrimp nets, and tanker traffic all the way up here from the Gulf of Mexico," he said. "One in a thousand."

Mimi groaned.

"Don't worry," said Mr. Prescott, gently touching the turtle. "See the little flicker of light in this one's eyes? That means there's hope. I haven't been wrong about that yet."

Before Mr. Prescott drove the turtle away, he promised to call when he heard any news.

Day after day, Mimi waited by the phone. Finally, exactly eight days, eighteen hours and thirty-three minutes later, he called to say the turtle was alive and resting peacefully at the New England Aquarium turtle rescue center south of Boston.

Mother promised to take Mimi for a visit.

Mrs. Sims shook her head and frowned. "You spend far too much time on that child," she said.

"Every turtle counts!" cried Mimi.

Mimi counted two days, one hour, and twenty minutes until they drove to see the turtle.

Penny, the Animal Care Director, led them to a crate marked "Ridley 3."

"If I name them, I get too attached," she said.

Mimi lay beside the crate for the whole afternoon. When her mother apologized, Penny said, "I understand. Sometimes I worry so much, I spend the night here with them."

"Every turtle counts," whispered Mimi.

"Exactly," said Penny.

When they came back the next Saturday, Penny tried to put Ridley 3 in the swimming pool.

But all Ridley 3 could do was float.

"Swim, Ridley 3. You can do it!" encouraged Penny.

"Row, row, row your boat," sang Mimi to Ridley 3.

But Ridley 3 didn't move.

"This doesn't look good," said Penny. "Without eating and without swimming, a turtle will not survive."

Mimi sang even louder.

"Let's try again," said Penny, placing the turtle in the pool. Mimi flapped her arms and splashed the water to try to teach Ridley 3 to swim.

Ridley 3 flapped and looked scared. Penny pulled Mimi back. "Ridley 3 has always lived in a big ocean, and doesn't like people getting too close."

Mimi knew exactly how that turtle felt.

"Here," said Penny, handing her some tongs with a bit of herring.
"See if you can get your turtle to eat."

Mimi moved the tongs slowly over the water. "Eat, turtle,"
she said, tickling the sides of its mouth.

Mimi's mother squeezed Penny's arm. It was the first time
Mimi had ever put her own sentence together.

Just then, so quickly they almost missed it, Ridley 3 chomped the herring, exhaled with a soft hiss, and dove to the bottom of the pool.

"Hooray!" cried Penny.

"Hooray!" shouted Mimi.

Around and around circled Ridley 3.

Around and around danced Mimi. "Ring around the rosie!" she sang, grabbing their hands.

Each Saturday, Ridley 3 was better. Mimi loved to lie by the pool and watch her turtle swim. She was always careful to leave plenty of room and to speak in a soft voice.

After fifteen Saturdays, it was time to say goodbye. The pool was needed for a sick harbor seal, so Ridley 3 would be flown to an aquarium in Florida before being released in warmer waters. Mimi held Ridley 3 very still while Penny clipped a tag on its right flipper.

"Will Ridley 3 make it home?" Mother asked.

"If she's female, she'll try to make it back in twenty to forty years to lay her eggs on the beach where she was born," said Penny.

"2034 to 2054," said Mimi automatically.

"What are her chances?" Mother asked in a shaky voice.

"Last year only four hundred turtles returned to Rancho Nuevo," said Penny. "Sixty years ago, there were 40,000."

Mimi traced her name in the turtle's tiny tag.

The next day, at exactly 3:12 p.m., Mother and Mimi ran to
the edge of the sea, waving and clapping at the plane overhead.
    "Goodbye and good luck, Ridley 3!" shouted Mother.
    "Goodbye and good luck, Ridley 3!" echoed Mimi.
    For just a moment, Mother hid her face in her mitten.
    Mimi reached over and patted her arm. "The turtle will
be all right, Mom."

Rancho Nuevo, Mexico, 2045

The grand arrival, or *arribada*, began under a full moon. No matter how many springs she had come, the sight of hundreds of sea turtles lumbering up the beach, drawn to a place they had abandoned decades and countless dangers earlier, amazed her.

Known as the autistic scientist who talked to turtles, she hiked the beach, counting each nesting mother and carefully recording how many had returned.

"Do you ever wonder why we spend so much time and money on a breed that might be meant to disappear?" asked her assistant.

A flash of silver caught her eye. She knelt down beside the turtle digging with its rear flippers. In silence, she traced the letters she had been seeking for so long and whispered, "Because every turtle counts."

AUTHOR'S NOTE

For 200 million years, sea turtles have roamed the oceans, surfacing only to lay their eggs. Today, just eight species survive, all on the brink of extinction. The rarest of these is the Kemp's ridley (*Lepidochelys kempii*), a breed which, until recently, hatched on only one small beach near Rancho Nuevo, Mexico. Sixty years ago, 40,000 turtle mothers nested each year at Rancho Nuevo. In recent years, that number has dropped below 400, due mainly to egg poachers, predators, and shrimp nets. Full grown at less than 100 pounds, the Kemp's ridley is the smallest of all sea turtles. Its feeding area spans the coastal waters from Texas to New England, with most adult ridleys migrating no further north than Chesapeake Bay. Between 1978 and 2006, the Mexican and U.S. governments cooperated in a head start program to rear and raise 23,987 Kemp's ridleys at the Galveston, Texas lab of the National Marine Fisheries Service. The first of these turtles recently returned to nest on the Texas coast.

Each summer, the youngest Kemp's ridleys wander as far as Massachusetts to feed on shellfish and herring in the rich waters off Cape Cod. They have survived sharks, nets, and tanker traffic to grow from the size of a dime to the size of a pie plate. When the water temperatures drop in Cape Cod Bay, some become confused as they try to migrate south and are blocked by land. Trapped on the north side of the Cape, the cold-blooded creatures lose body heat as the water temperature drops. For a short period in November and December, the comatose, "cold-stunned" turtles drift to the beaches of the Cape's north coast. Thanks to the efforts of the Massachusetts Audubon Society, the New England Aquarium, and a host of turtle rescue facilities from Massachusetts to Florida, many of the cold-stunned turtles are rescued, rehabilitated, and relocated.

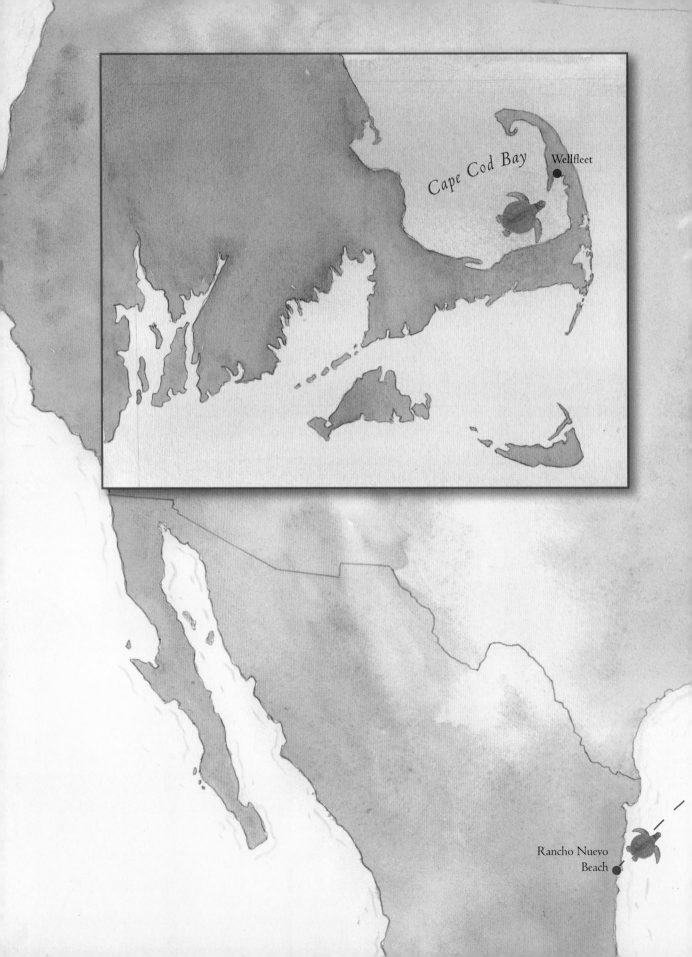

Cape Cod Bay

Wellfleet

Rancho Nuevo
Beach